This book belongs to:

For Sarah and Simon
for making me laugh, making me write
and most importantly
making me tea

L.M.G.

For Lizzie, Abbie
and Andrew

R.S.

First published in 2008 by Meadowside Children's Books
185 Fleet Street London EC4A 2HS
www.meadowsidebooks.com

Illustrations © Rachel Swirles
The right of Rachel Swirles to be identified as the illustrator
of this work has been asserted by her in accordance with
the Copyright, Designs and Patents Act, 1988

A CIP catalogue record for this book
is available from the British Library
10 9 8 7 6 5 4 3 2 1
Printed in Indonesia

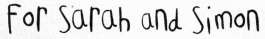

meadowside
CHILDREN'S BOOKS

thumbelina

Retold by Lucy M George and illustrated by Rachel Swirles

there was once a tiny little girl who was no bigger than a thumb. She was called Thumbelina.

She lived in a beautiful flower in a warm and happy house.

On bright mornings she would row across the milk bowl, with a whistle and a giggle as she went, smiling and happy with the world.

But one day,
as she slept beside
the window…

...a nasty toad mother
crept up and snatched her!

She trapped Thumbelina on a
lily leaf, too small to swim home,
too afraid to call for help.

The toad mother was going
to make Thumbelina marry
her horrid toad son!

As Thumbelina's tears splashed
into the pool, the fish looked up
and saw how lovely she was.
They had to help.

So they nibbled and they gnawed
through the stem of the lily,
until the leaf floated free.

"Oh thank you, thank you!"
she called as she floated away.

But as she drifted, she realised
that she was going further
and further away
from her home.

uddenly, a mayfly landed on her leaf. Without even saying 'hello', it poked her and said, "My, my! You are a pretty little thing, I think I shall take you back to my family."

"Oooh! It has no wings," said the mother.

"Ergh!
It has no feelers,"
said the brother.

"Yuk!
It only has two feet,"
said the sister,
"and it is so ugly!"

They cast Thumbelina
from their tree.

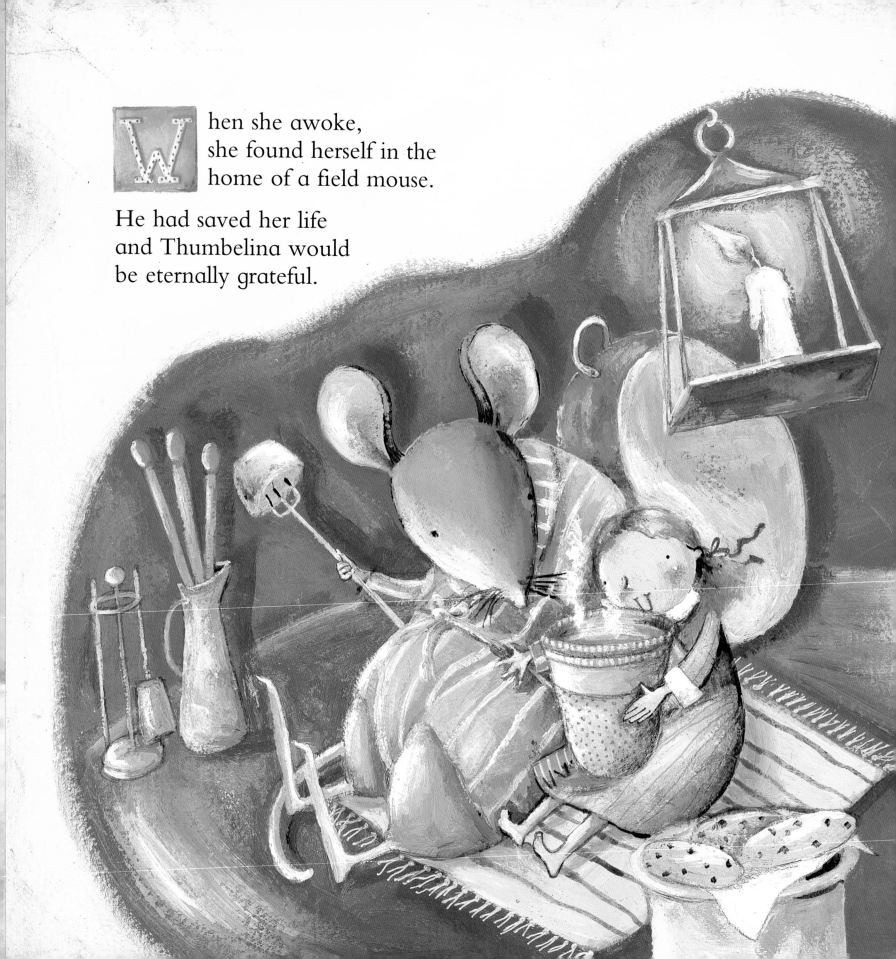

W hen she awoke,
she found herself in the
home of a field mouse.

He had saved her life
and Thumbelina would
be eternally grateful.

She and Mouse spent the whole winter
together, happy in his cosy little home.
Beside the merry little fire they were safe and
warm from the frosty winds outside.

t hat winter, Thumbelina would walk with Mouse to visit his friend Mole every afternoon for a cup of tea and homemade cakes.

They had a splendid time and Mole began to grow rather fond of Thumbelina.

Mole

Mouse was so kind to Thumbelina, but she soon found that he wanted her to repay him. The following year, Thumbelina would have to go and live with Mole in his dark underground hole!

And she didn't.

But she missed him. And since
he had gone, Thumbelina had spent
all of her days inside with Mouse.
And now, the time had come to go
and live with Mole in his
dark underground hole.

Thumbelina
longed to see the sky
one more time, so she crept out
early one morning
whilst the ground was still soft.

A tear rolled down her cheek.
"Goodbye flowers!" she said sadly.

Suddenly, a bird landed beside her.
"Why are you crying?" he asked.
"Because," she wept, not looking up,
"I have to marry an old, blind mole tomorrow
and I'll have to live underground forever…"

He smiled and then, laughing gently, he said…

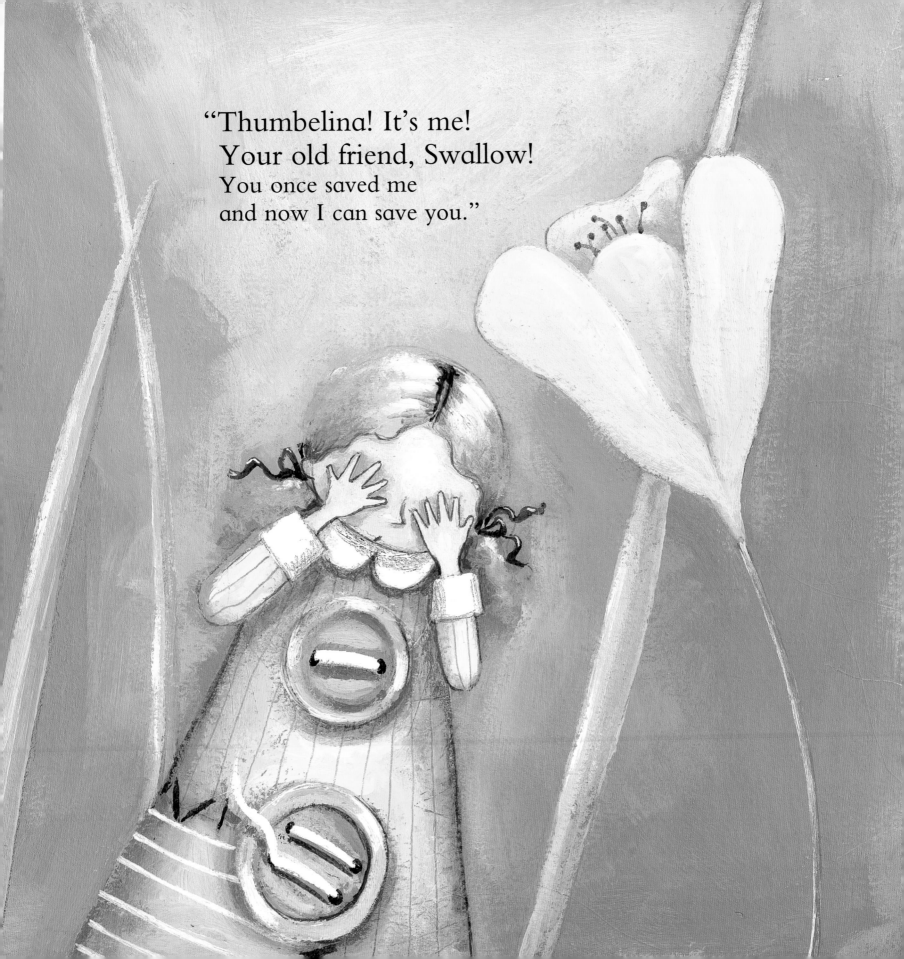

"Thumbelina! It's me!
Your old friend, Swallow!
You once saved me
and now I can save you."

As they swooped towards the ground,
Thumbelina saw a beautiful
white flower.

"That one!" she pointed.

But as she fell softly into the flower,
Thumbelina gave a little cry of surprise.
For right there, in the middle was...

The Prince
of the Fairies!

Swallow waved goodbye
with a promise to visit her
every spring.

And so, at last,
Thumbelina had found
her home.